YiDDiSH
SAVES THE DAY!

by Debbie Levy

Illustrated by Hector Borlasca

APPLES & HONEY PRESS

For my Yiddish keepers—my grandmother, Rose Kleinert Salzberg, whose Polish-Yiddish lilt still makes me smile, and my in-laws, Libby and Burton Hoffman.
—DL

To my wife, Silvana, and my daughter, Micaela
—HB

For ease of reading, the spelling of Yiddish words in this book generally follows familiar, popular usage, rather than the standardized system created by the YIVO Institute for Jewish Research. And a note on pronunciation: when you see the letter combination CH (as in chutzpah and mishpocha), don't think CH as in CHair or LunCH. Instead, make a sound as if you're clearing your throat. That's CH.)

Apples & Honey Press
An imprint of Behrman House
www.applesandhoneypress.com

ISBN 978-1-68115-544-9

Library of Congress Cataloging-in-Publication Data
Names: Levy, Debbie, author. | Borlasca, Hector, illustrator.
Title: Yiddish saves the day! / by Debbie Levy ; illustrated by Hector Borlasca.
Description: [Milburn, NJ] : Apples & Honey Press, an imprint of Behrman
   House, [2019] | Summary: When a boy loses the notebook of interesting
   words he collected for school, his extended family supplies a long list of
   Yiddish words to replace them. Includes pronunciations and definitions.
Identifiers: LCCN 2018015158 | ISBN 9781681155449
Subjects: | CYAC: Stories in rhyme. | Yiddish language—Fiction. |
   Jews—United States—Fiction. | Family life—Fiction. |
   Vocabulary—Fiction.
Classification: LCC PZ8.3.L5777 Yid 2019 | DDC [E]—dc23 LC record
   available at https://lccn.loc.gov/2018015158

The illustrations were created using digital tools, pencil and acrylic paint.

Design by Anne Redmond
Edited by Ann D. Koffsky
Printed in the United States of America

9 8 7 6 5 4 3 2 1

When your walk home from school is unusually bad,

Don't be **BROYGES**,

discouraged—

don't even be sad.

broyges (*BROY-guhs*): angry

Announce to the house: "**OY**, did I have a **SHLEP**!

I fell on my **SHNOZ** when my foot missed a step!

I tripped like a **KLUTZ** and lost my left shoe!

oy (*OY*) or **oy vey** (*OY VAY*): oh! or oh, woe!

shlep (*SHLEP*): A difficult trip

shnoz (*SHNAHZ*): nose

klutz (*KLUHTS*): clumsy person

tuches (*TUCH-is*): butt

And, **OY VEY**, my **TUCHES**!

I fell on that, too!"

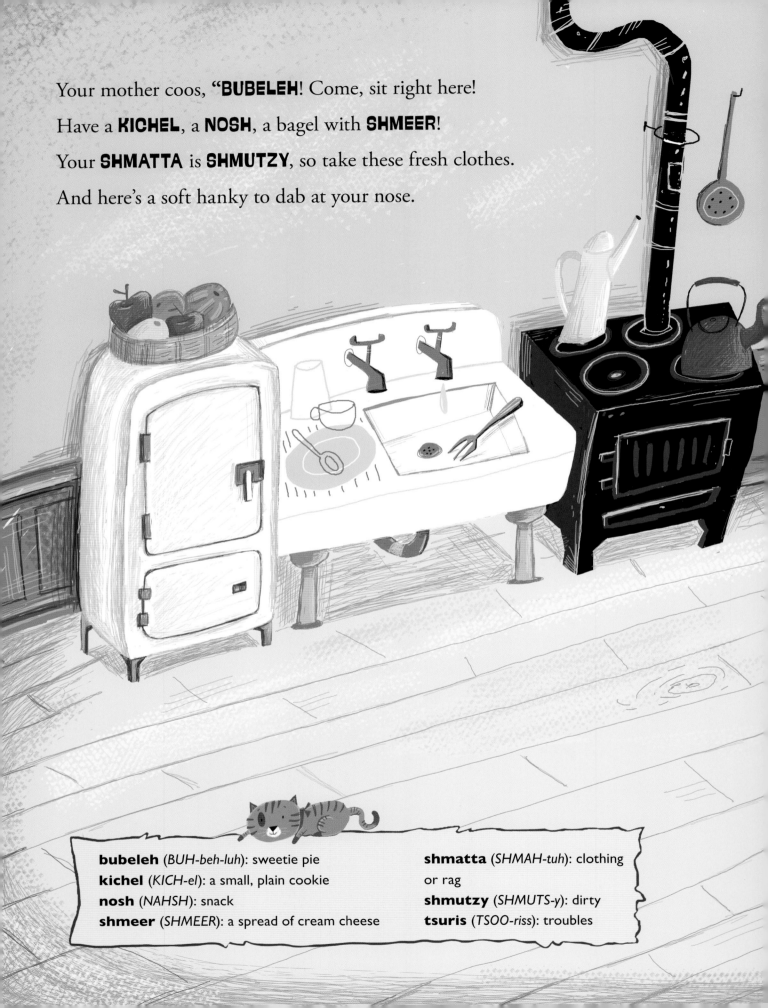

Your mother coos, "**BUBELEH**! Come, sit right here!

Have a **KICHEL**, a **NOSH**, a bagel with **SHMEER**!

Your **SHMATTA** is **SHMUTZY**, so take these fresh clothes.

And here's a soft hanky to dab at your nose.

bubeleh (*BUH-beh-luh*): sweetie pie
kichel (*KICH-el*): a small, plain cookie
nosh (*NAHSH*): snack
shmeer (*SHMEER*): a spread of cream cheese

shmatta (*SHMAH-tuh*): clothing
or rag
shmutzy (*SHMUTS-y*): dirty
tsuris (*TSOO-riss*): troubles

Now, tell me your **TSURIS**—all of your troubles!

Have some cold juice. Here's a straw to make bubbles!"

Later you notice—your notebook is gone!

The one with the words that your test will be on!

"**GEVALT**!" you exclaim. "I'm such a **SHLEMIEL**!"

You're **FARTOOTST** and **TSEDOODELT**,

but, look, here's the deal . . .

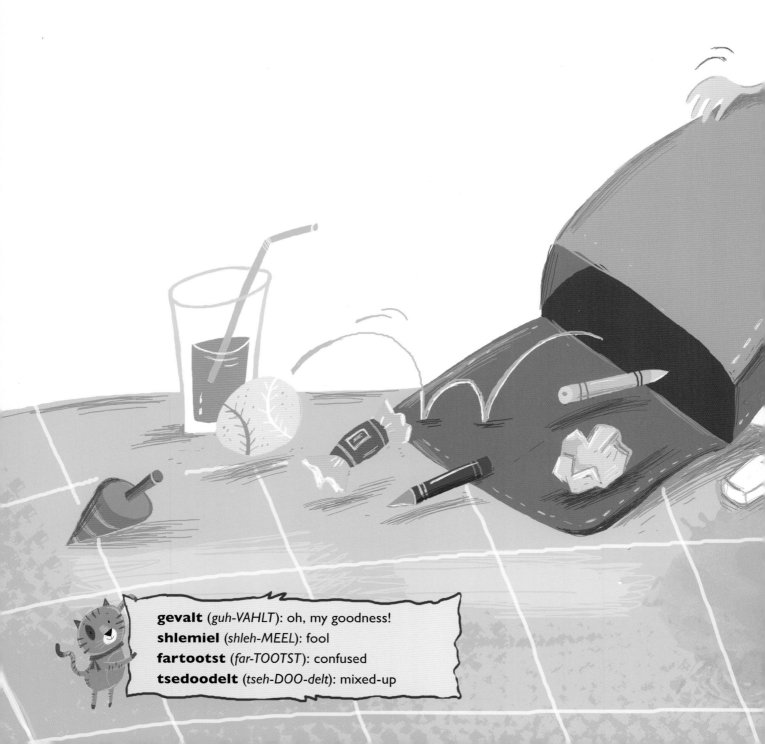

gevalt (*guh-VAHLT*): oh, my goodness!
shlemiel (*shleh-MEEL*): fool
fartootst (*far-TOOTST*): confused
tsedoodelt (*tseh-DOO-delt*): mixed-up

No notebook? Bad **MAZEL**!

But not all *that* bad.

Bad is a **GOLEM** who's grouchy and mad!

mazel (*MAH-zel*): luck
golem (*GO-lem*): supernatural being
dybbuk (*DIB-uhk*): ghoul, ghost

Bad is a **DYBBUK** who gives you a curse!

See what I mean? Things could be worse!

Next thing you know, there's a knock at the door.

It's your uncles and aunts, and cousins galore.

The entire **MISHPOCHA**! They jabber and **SHMOOZE**.

They joke and they **KIBITZ** and catch up on news.

mishpocha (*mish-PAW-chuh*): family
shmooze (*SHMOOZ*): chitchat
kibitz (*KIB-its*): to joke
nu (*NEW*): so?

Your aunt wants to know,
"**NU**, what's doing with you?"
You tell her: the notebook,
the test, and the shoe . . .

Your teacher asked all of the **KINDER** to bring
new words into class that have sizzle and zing.
She'll choose the best ones to include on the test—
words that show spirit and **CHUTZPAH** and zest.

kinder (*KIN*-der): children
chutzpah (*CHUTS-puh*): nerve
kop (*CUP*): head, mind

In the notebook that's lost you collected some words—
but they've flown from your **KOP** like a flock of fast birds!

Dinnertime! You **ESS**—a **BISSEL** too much,

KNAIDELS and **KUGELS** and **KNISHES** and such.

"My **KISHKES** are bursting! I'm **PLOTZING**!" you groan.

"**FEH**, how I **FRESSED**! What a **CHAZZER**!" you moan.

With all of that **KVETCHING**, you start to feel well!

A **SHPRITZ** of club soda—you're perfectly swell!

ess (*ESS*): eat

bissel (*BIH-sul*): a little

knaidel (*kuh-NAY-dul*): dumpling, often made of matzah meal and served in chicken soup

kugel (*KOO-guhl*): pudding of noodles or potatoes

knish (*kuh-NISH*): small pastry filled with potatoes, meat, or other savory filling

Your cousin calls out, "Give a **KUK** what I found . . ."

kishkes (*KISH-kehs*): guts

plotz (*PLAHTS*): burst

feh (*FEH*): ugh!

fress (*FRESS*): eat a lot

chazzer (*CHAH-zur*): pig

kvetch (*KVETCH*): complain

shpritz (*SHPRITS*): squirt

kuk (*KOOK*): look

. . . It's your shoe! Look—he spied it outside on the ground!

"What a **MENSCH**!" you applaud him, and he starts to **KVELL**.

If your notebook shows up, then all will be well!

mensch (*MENSH*): a fine person
kvell (*KVELL*): to gush with pride
mazel (*MAH-zel*): luck
Yiddish (*YID-ish*): this language

"This is good **MAZEL**!" the relatives say.

"See how your luck changed from *bad* to *okay*?"

"But I still need my words," you fret, "words for my test!"

"You need **YIDDISH**!" they laugh, and then they suggest . . .

. . . such a long list of words—and what they all mean—
you're writing them down like a language machine.
Words you know well! Words you *never* have seen!
Some are big, some are small, some are words in between!

TSURIS and **TUCHES**,

SHMATTA and **SHMOOZE**,

you've got words on your tongue that the whole world can use.

With **BUBELEH**, **CHUTZPAH**, **FARTOOTST**, and **GEVALT**,

your list is a treasure—like jewels in a vault!

"This was so **HAIMISH**!" the relatives cry.

"Thanks for your help! **ZEI GEZUNDT**!" you reply.

With your new list of words, your worry is gone.

You **SHLOF** like a baby, from darkness to dawn!

haimish (*HAY-mish*): homey, cozy
zei gezundt (*ZYE geh-ZUNT*): be healthy! goodbye!
shlof (*SHLOF*): sleep

Next morning you hand in your **YIDDISHA** list.

The teacher beams: "These are words I would have missed!

They're just what we need to spice up our lessons—

mighty, **MESHUGGENEH**, super expressions!

By the way—you earn an A+ on the test!

With **YIDDISH** all things have

turned out for the best!

TSURIS
SHMOOZE
TUCHES
FARTOOTST

GEVALT

meshuggeneh (*meh-SHUH-geh-nuh*): wacky,
ridiculous
Yiddisha (*YID-ish-eh*): Jewish

So whenever your day's heading into a slide,

remember—there's **CHUTZPAH**! and **FEH**! on your side.

With Yiddish, a laugh is a **KIBITZ** away,

and its **super word power** could—

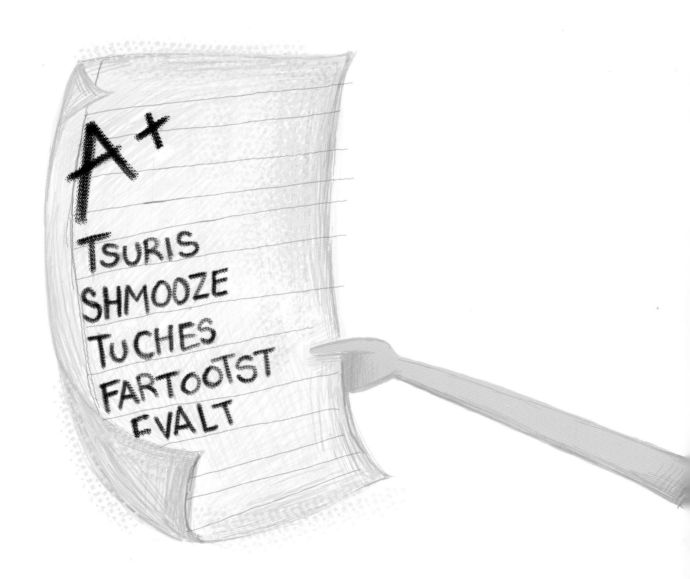

A+

TSURIS
SHMOOZE
TUCHES
FARTOOTST
GVALT

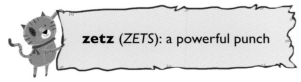

zetz (ZETS): a powerful punch

ZETZ! —save the day!

Now—look in the closet,
under a glove . . .

mazel tov (*MAH-zel tov*):
congratulations

. . . a lost-and-found notebook.

OY VEY! MAZEL TOV!

A NOTE FOR FAMILIES

Okay: maybe in real life Yiddish doesn't make everything better. But Yiddish words—like the ones in this story—are so powerful, and so often comical, they're like the superheroes of language!

No one is sure exactly when, how, and where Yiddish began, but many experts say it developed a thousand years ago as Jewish people in Europe combined the local languages of the places where they settled with languages their ancestors had spoken in other lands. By the 1800s, millions of Jews around the world spoke Yiddish. Writers created stories, poems, songs, plays, books, and newspapers in Yiddish. The result was a rich and vibrant culture. Today, far fewer people speak it, but many Yiddish words have found their way into the everyday speech of Jews and non-Jews alike. When you hear someone say a strong, funny, or expressive word—like **CHUTZPAH**, **SHLEP**, **KVELL**, or **KLUTZ**—the speaker may not know it's Yiddish, but you will!

May *you* become a **YIDDISH MAVEN**!

Debbie

maven (*MAY-vin*): expert